SOUTHGATE PUBL

3 9082 06428025 1

DATE DUE	
SEP 2 5 1998	MAY 0 2 2001
MAR 0 3 1999	AUG 0 8 2001
	AUG 2 9 2001
JUL 0 6 1999	JAN 1 9 2002
DEC 1 3 1999	APR 1 8 2002
FEB 1 6 2000	MAR 3 0 2007
MAR 0 2 2001	FEB 28 2013
APR / 3 2001	JUN 1 1 2014
	APR 0 9 2018

Picture
JE

COPY 14

Hayes, Geoffrey.
    Patrick and Ted / Geoffrey Hayes. --
New York : Four Winds Press, c1984.
    unp. : ill.   bk1 PreS-1
    SUMMARY: Best friends, Patrick and
Ted, find their relationship strained
when Ted goes away for the summer and
Patrick finds other activities and
friends to occupy his time.
    ISBN 0-590-07902-6 : 5.95

                                        71589

    1.Friendship--Fiction.

SOUTHGATE PUBLIC LIBRARY   S84
14680 DIX-TOLEDO ROAD   dc 19
SOUTHGATE, MI 48195   AACR2   83-18486
                                  CIP MARC AC

ЯАЯВІJ
LIBRARY

PATRICK

and

TED

PATRICK

and

TED

Geoffrey Hayes

Four Winds Press
New York

DEC 1 3 1988

3 9082 06428025 1

Copyright © 1984 by Geoffrey Hayes.
All rights reserved. No part of this publication may be reproduced,
stored in a retrieval system, or transmitted, in any form or by any means,
electronic, mechanical, photocopying, recording, or otherwise, without prior
written permission from the Publisher. Published by Four Winds Press,
A Division of Scholastic Inc., 730 Broadway, New York, N.Y. 10003.
Manufactured in the United States of America

10 9 8 7 6 5 4 3 2 1

The text of this book is set in 16 pt. Horley Old Style.
The illustrations are halftone drawings with overlays,
prepared by the artist for black, red, yellow, and blue.

Library of Congress Cataloging in Publication Data
Hayes, Geoffrey.
Patrick and Ted.
Summary: Best friends, Patrick and Ted, find their
relationship strained when Ted goes away for the
summer and Patrick finds other activities and friends
to occupy his time.
[1. Friendship—Fiction.   2. Bears—Fiction]   I. Title.
PZ7.H31455Par   1984   [E]   83-18486
ISBN 0-590-07902-6

SOUTHGATE PUBLIC LIBRARY
14680 DIX-TOLEDO ROAD
SOUTHGATE, MI 48195

For Kal,
and the memory of "Racer"

SOUTHGATE PUBLIC LIBRARY
14680 DIX-TOLEDO ROAD
SOUTHGATE, MI 48195

Patrick and Ted went everywhere together.
Their favorite place was beneath a big
tree in Patrick's backyard.

They spent whole mornings there,
building hideouts and sharing secrets.

Sometimes they argued over toys, or about which games to play,

but it did not matter...

because Ted was Patrick's best friend,
and Patrick was Ted's.

They were like brothers, and nobody ever
thought of one without thinking of
the other.

Then, one summer Ted went to stay
with his aunt and uncle at
their farm in the hills.

After he left, Patrick had no one to build
things with, no one to tell secrets to.

But as the days went by,

he began to play with the other kids and
found that he enjoyed being just Patrick.

He went to the movies with Mama Bear.

He made a rocket ship
from soap cartons.

He rode his new scooter to a hideout
of his own.

In the fall, Ted returned with two pet geese, a present from his aunt and uncle.

They were loud and quick, and Patrick
did not like them.

Patrick showed Ted his new scooter and how
to make it zoom around corners. But
Ted grabbed it away from him.

BONK!

STUPID PIECE OF JUNK!

Patrick got angry and pushed Ted
against their hideout.

Patrick and Ted fixed their hideout
and spent the rest of the morning
playing games and sharing secrets.

From that day on, Patrick and Ted
no longer did everything together,
but it did not matter,

because Ted was still Patrick's best friend,
and Patrick was Ted's.